THE
SHERLOCK HOLMES

CHILDREN'S COLLECTION

CREATURES, CODES AND CURIOUS CASES

Published by Sweet Cherry Publishing Limited
Unit 36, Vulcan House,
Vulcan Road,
Leicester, LE5 3EF
United Kingdom

First published in the UK in 2021
2021 edition

2 4 6 8 10 9 7 5 3 1

ISBN: 978-1-78226-438-5

Sherlock Holmes: The Creeping Man

Cover design by Arianna Bellucci and Amy Booth
Illustrations by Arianna Bellucci

Lexile® code numerical measure L = Lexile® 710L

www.sweetcherrypublishing.com

Printed and bound in India
I.TP002

SHERLOCK HOLMES

THE CREEPING MAN

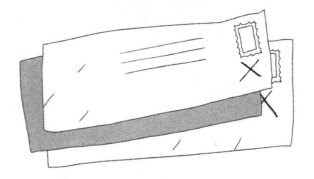

SIR ARTHUR CONAN DOYLE

Chapter One

One Sunday evening in September, I received an urgent message from Sherlock Holmes.

If convenient, come to Baker Street at once.
If inconvenient, come anyway.

Holmes

I smiled to myself.

Holmes had very set habits – playing his violin, smoking his pipe and reading his reference books. Seeing me was another.

Sometimes I was able to help Holmes in his work. I could tell him if someone was sick, treat them if they were wounded or occasionally even work out how they died. Other times he just needed me to sit with him as he sorted through a mystery in his mind.

When I arrived at 221B Baker Street that evening, Holmes was curled up in his armchair, smoking his pipe and frowning in thought.

I could see that he was in the middle of a tough problem. He didn't speak, but waved a hand at my old chair and I sat down.

We sat in silence for almost half an hour. Then, as suddenly as if he had woken from a dream, Holmes looked up at me and smiled.

'Excuse my daydreaming, Watson,' he said. 'I have been given some strange facts recently. I've been thinking a lot about dogs.

I may write an article on the use of dogs in detective work.'

'But surely, Holmes, that has already been done,' I said. 'Bloodhounds–'

'No, no, Watson, everyone knows about bloodhounds. There is another way that dogs can help detectives that is not so obvious. You see, a dog reflects family life. You rarely find a happy dog in a miserable family or a sad dog in a happy one. Snarling people have snarling dogs, and dangerous people have dangerous dogs. It's nothing to do with the breed. It's all about how they're raised.'

I opened my mouth to speak, but Holmes jumped in. 'It's all connected to the case I have been given,' he said. 'It's a mystery like a tangled ball of string, and I'm looking for the loose end. The first question is this: why did Professor Presbury's faithful and happy dog, Roy, bite him?'

I sighed and sank back in my chair. Had Holmes sent for me just to talk about dogs?

Holmes glanced across at me.

'The same old Watson!' he said. 'You'll never learn. How many times have I told you that the biggest mysteries can be solved by looking at the tiniest details? You must have heard of Professor Presbury, Watson. He teaches at the university in Camford. His wolfhound has suddenly started attacking him. What do you make of it?'

'The dog is sick,' I suggested.

'Well, maybe, but he doesn't attack anyone else. And he doesn't always attack the professor – only sometimes. It's curious, Watson. Very curious.'

There was a ring at the front door.

'Ah, young Mr Bennett is early,' said Holmes. 'I had hoped to chat with you for longer before he came.'

I heard the sound of footsteps on the stairs, and then Mrs Hudson, our housekeeper, showed Mr Bennett in. He was a tall, handsome young man of about thirty, very well dressed and elegant. He looked very nervous.

Mr Bennett shook hands with Holmes and then stared at me in surprise.

'This matter is very personal, Mr Holmes,' he said, almost in a whisper. 'I really can't talk about it in front of another person.'

'Have no fear, Mr Bennett,' said Holmes, smiling. 'Doctor Watson is very discreet. He will never repeat what he's about to hear. And I am likely to need his assistance in the case.'

'All right, Mr Holmes. If you insist,' said Mr Bennett.

Holmes turned to me. 'Watson, this gentleman, Mr Trevor Bennett, is assistant to the great scientist, Professor Presbury. He lives in the professor's house and is engaged to his daughter. Mr Bennett has become very worried about his employer.'

Mr Bennett nodded. 'Does Doctor Watson know why I'm worried?' he asked.

'I have not had time to explain,' said Holmes.

'Then perhaps I had better repeat the story before telling you about some new events. But I warn you, Doctor Watson, this may be one of the strangest things you have ever heard.'

Chapter Two

'I doubt this will be the strangest thing Watson has heard,' Holmes chuckled. 'He has heard of some very odd things during our work together. But I'd like to tell the story myself, Mr Bennet, if that's all right? Just to make sure I have all the details in the correct order.'

Mr Bennet nodded, and Holmes began: 'The professor has a great reputation in Europe, Watson. He is an impressive scientist. His wife is dead and he has one daughter called Edith. He's also a very strong, fit man for sixty-one years old.

'A few months ago, he became engaged to Alice Morphy, the daughter of Mr Morphy, his colleague at the university. Alice Morphy is in her early twenties, so is much younger than Professor Presbury. This caused the professor's family to disapprove of the marriage.'

'We thought the age gap too big,' added Mr Bennett.

'Oh, it's natural for you to worry,' said Holmes. 'But Alice seems to be very much in love with the professor.'

Holmes leaned towards me. I could see the excitement in his eyes. 'After his engagement,' he went on, 'the professor did something he had never done before: he left home without saying where he was going. He was away for two weeks. He would not tell anyone where he had been, which is odd since he is a very honest, open man.

'By chance, Mr Bennett received a letter from a friend in Prague, who said that he had seen

Professor Presbury out there, but was not able to speak to him.

'Now comes the point of the story,' went on Holmes. 'Since the professor returned from Prague a curious change has come over him. He has changed so much that his family and friends wondered for a moment whether he were a different man – perhaps an identical twin. He is still just as clever, and his lectures are as brilliant as ever, but there

is something new about him –
something sinister and dangerous.

'His daughter, Mr Bennett's
fiancée, has tried again and again
to remind the professor of the
father he used to be. But it is as if
he's wearing a mask that is hiding
his true self.

'And then there are the letters,'
Holmes said. 'Please tell us about
them, Mr Bennett.'

Mr Bennett looked at me. 'You
must understand, Doctor Watson,

that the professor has no secrets from me. He treats me like a son. Well, he used to, at least. As his secretary, I used to open and sort all his letters. But after he returned from Prague, this changed. He told me that certain letters might come from London that would be marked with a cross under the stamp. He said

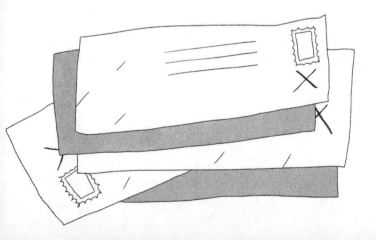

that I was not allowed to open them, and should put them to one side for him to read.

'Several letters like that arrived. The handwriting was very messy, almost unreadable. If the professor was replying to them, then he was doing so in secret. As there were no outgoing letters in the basket where we put our mail for posting.'

'And what about the box?' said Holmes.

'Ah, yes, the box,' said Mr Bennett. 'The professor brought back a little wooden box from his travels. It is a carved wooden box, like those you see in Germany. He keeps it in his instrument cupboard, where he stores his tools and chemicals. One day I was looking for a microscope and I picked up the box. To my

surprise, the professor got very angry and shouted at me for touching it. It was the first time anything like that had happened, and I was very upset.'

Mr Bennett took a little book out of his pocket. 'That was on the 2nd of July,' he said.

'You are like a detective yourself, Mr Bennett,' said Holmes, smiling. 'I may need more of those dates you have noted.'

'From the moment he began to act strangely, I made notes of everything – every date, every odd occurrence,' said Mr Bennett. 'So I know that it was on the 2nd of July that Roy the dog attacked the professor as he walked from his study into the hall. It happened again on the 11th of July, and then again on the 20th of July. After that we had to put Roy in the stables. He sleeps out there with the horses now. It's

such a shame. He was such a
dear, loving animal – but I think I
am boring you, Mr Holmes.'

It was clear to both Mr
Bennett and myself that Holmes
was not listening. He was gazing

at the ceiling
with a blank
expression on
his face.

'Strange. Most strange,' Holmes murmured to himself. 'But didn't you say that something even stranger happened, Mr Bennet?'

Mr Bennett's face clouded over as if he were remembering something horrible.

'What I am going to tell you now happened two nights ago,' he said. 'I was lying awake at about two o'clock in the morning when I heard a dull, shuffling sound coming from the hallway.

I opened my door and peeped out.'

'What date was that?' asked Holmes.

Mr Bennett seemed annoyed at the interruption. 'I have said, sir, that it was the night before last, the 4th of September.'

Holmes nodded and smiled. 'So you did,' he said and waved his hand for Mr Bennett to continue.

Mr Bennett cleared his throat. 'It was a really terrifying experience, Mr Holmes,' he said.

'I don't scare easily, but I was scared by what I saw.'

Mr Bennett paused again and clasped his hands together. There was silence in our sitting room except for the muffled sound of hooves outside in the street. Holmes and I waited, holding our breaths, for our visitor to continue.

Chapter Three

'The hallway was dark except for a glimmer of moonlight shining through one window,' continued Mr Bennett. 'I could see that something was coming towards my bedroom. Then it stepped into the moonlight and I saw that it was the professor. But he was crawling, Mr Holmes. Crawling!

'He was not quite on his hands and knees, but more on his hands and feet. He looked so strange, yet he seemed to move easily. I was so shocked that I couldn't move.

It was not until he had reached my door that I was able to step forwards and ask if he needed help.

'His answer was extraordinary. He sprang up, spat out a terrible word to me, and then hurried down the stairs. I waited for about an hour, but he did not come back. It must have been daylight before he returned to his room.'

Holmes turned to me. 'Well, Watson, what do you think of that?' he asked.

'A bad back, possibly,' I said. 'I have known people with very sore backs to walk just like that, and it would certainly make the person irritable.'

'Good, Watson! You always think of the most sensible answer. It can't be right, however, because the professor was able to stand upright just seconds afterwards.'

'He is very healthy,' said Mr Bennett. 'In fact, he looks stronger than he has been in years.

But those are the facts, Mr Holmes. I can't go to the police because no crime has been committed. Edith and I are utterly at our wits' end. We don't know what to do, but we cannot stand around and do nothing.'

'It is certainly a very curious case,' said Holmes. 'What do you think, Watson?'

'Speaking as a doctor, I think Professor Presbury needs counselling,' I said. 'Perhaps his family not approving of his fiancée, Alice Morphy, has caused him a lot of stress and affected his mind. Maybe he went to Prague to try to free himself from it. The letters and the box may be to do with some business he did while he was there. Some new scientific research, perhaps.'

'And the dog disagreed with the business deals?' Holmes laughed. 'No, no, Watson, there is more to it than that. I can only suggest ...'

Holmes was interrupted by the
door opening. A young lady was
shown into the room.

As she appeared, Mr Bennett
sprang up and ran forwards with
his hands out to meet hers.

'Edith, dear! Nothing's the matter, I hope?'

'Oh, Jack, I have been so frightened!' said the lady. 'It's awful to be there alone.'

'Mr Holmes and Doctor Watson, this is my fiancée, Miss Edith Presbury,' said Mr Bennett.

'We had realised that already, hadn't we, Watson?' said Holmes with a smile. 'Has something else happened that we should know about, Miss Presbury?'

Miss Edith Presbury had a bright, kind face. She smiled at Holmes and I as she sat down next to Mr Bennett.

'I came to London to find Mr Bennett,' she explained. 'When I heard that he had left the hotel, I guessed he had come here to see you, Mr Holmes. I couldn't stay in the house without him any longer. Not with my father acting in the strange way that he is – especially after what happened last night.

Oh, Mr Holmes, what do you think about my poor father?'

'The case is still a mystery to me. But perhaps what you have to say will help a little.'

Miss Presbury nodded and said: 'Yesterday, Father was acting very strangely, walking about the house as if he were in a dream. He didn't seem to know who he was. Then last night, well ...' her voice trailed off.

'Tell me what happened,' said Holmes.

Chapter Four

'I was woken in the night by the dog barking furiously. Poor Roy is chained up by the stables now.

'My room is on the second floor, and I always sleep with my bedroom door locked now because I am worried that my father may do something awful. Last night I left the blind up.

When I awoke, I lay staring at
the full moon as it shone through
the window, and was listening
to Roy's barking. Suddenly, my
father's face appeared on the
other side.

'I thought I might die of surprise and horror, Mr Holmes. How had he climbed up there? Surely it was impossible. Yet there was his face, pressed against the glass, and he had one hand raised as if he were going to open the window. I was terrified. I couldn't move. For about twenty seconds, I stared at his face. Then it vanished.

'I couldn't sleep after that. I lay cold and shivering, and staring at the window until morning.

At breakfast, Father was in a horrible temper. He did not mention what had happened during the night. I didn't either, but I made an excuse to come into London to get away from him.'

I glanced at Holmes' face. He looked surprised at Miss Presbury's story.

'My dear young lady,' he said, 'you say your room is on the second floor. Is there a long ladder in the garden?'

'No, Mr Holmes, that's the amazing part of it. There is no possible way of reaching the window. And yet he was there. It was as if he had sprouted wings.'

'And the date was the 5th of September,' said Holmes. 'That certainly makes it more complicated.'

Now it was Miss Presbury who looked surprised.

'This is the second time you have mentioned the date,

Mr Holmes,' said Mr Bennett. 'Do you think it's important to the case?'

'I think it may be,' said Holmes. 'But I'm not yet sure why.'

'Are you thinking of how the phases of the moon can affect people's minds?' asked Mr Bennett.

'No, certainly not.' Holmes chuckled. 'And I don't think he's a werewolf either. No, it's something quite different. Could

you leave your
notebook with
me, Mr Bennet,
and I'll check
the dates?'

Mr Bennet nodded.

'Now, Watson, I think it's
clear what we must do,' Holmes
continued. 'This young lady has
told us that her father doesn't
seem to remember what he
did on certain dates. We will
therefore visit the professor

and tell him that he gave us an appointment during one of the days he cannot remember. He will think it's the fault of his memory that he doesn't remember our appointment. That way, we shall have a good close look at him.'

'That is excellent,' said Mr Bennett. 'But I warn you that Professor Presbury is irritable and violent at times.'

Holmes smiled. 'I understand. But if my theories are correct, then it is very important that we visit him immediately. Tomorrow we shall be in Camford, Mr Bennett. I believe there is an inn called Chequers there that is quite pleasant.'

Holmes turned to me. 'Pack your bags, Watson. We shall be away for the next few days.'

Chapter Five

The next morning, I met Holmes at King's Cross Station and we boarded a train for Camford.

While I was excited to be working on another case with Holmes, I felt bad about having to abandon my patients at such short notice. Nevertheless, I tried to enjoy the pretty scenery on the journey.

We got out at Camford and made our way to the Chequers Inn to leave our luggage. Only then did Holmes talk about the case we were investigating.

'I think, Watson, that we can catch Professor Presbury before he has his lunch. He lectures at the university at eleven o'clock each morning and then goes home.'

'Right. What's our story then? Which day shall we say that

we booked the
appointment with
him?' I asked.

Holmes
glanced at Mr
Bennett's notebook.

'The 26th of August. It says
here that the professor had one
of his strange episodes then. So
we will assume that his memories
from that day are a little hazy.
Are your acting skills up to the
task, Watson?'

'I'll try,' I said, feeling a little nervous.

'Excellent, Watson!'

We hailed a cab and gave the driver the address. Then we swept past a row of ancient colleges and finally turned into a tree-lined driveway. We stopped at the door of a charming house surrounded by neat green lawns. The walls of the house were covered with ivy and late-blooming wisteria flowers.

As we climbed out of the cab,
I saw someone watching us from
the window. He had grizzled grey
hair, very sharp eyes that sat
under bushy eyebrows

and he wore thick-rimmed reading glasses.

A moment later a servant opened the door and showed us into the professor's study.

The professor didn't look strange or eccentric in any way. He was a tall, well-built man with a strong face and stern expression. He wore a frock-coat that made him look exactly like what he was: a dignified university lecturer. His eyes were his most remarkable feature. They were keen, observant and clever.

The professor looked at Holmes' business card. 'Please sit down, gentlemen. What can I do for you?'

Holmes smiled in a friendly way. 'That was the question I was about to ask you, Professor.'

'Ask *me*, sir?' Professor Presbury said.

'Perhaps there is some mistake. I had a letter saying that Professor Presbury of Camford needed my services. It said that you would like an appointment with me,' said Holmes.

'Oh, really?' asked the professor. A malicious sparkle glittered in his intense grey eyes. 'You had a letter, did you? May I ask from whom?'

'From you, Professor,' said Holmes.

'From me? Really?' said the professor with a laugh.

'Yes,' said Holmes. 'But if I have made a mistake, there is no harm done. I can only say that I am sorry.'

'Not at all,' said the professor. 'I would like to know more about this matter. When did I write this letter?

'It was dated the 26th of August,' said Holmes.

The professor looked sternly at Holmes. 'The 26th, you say? Do you have this letter with you to prove what you say?'

'No, I have not,' said Holmes.

'I see,' said the professor, and then he walked across the room and rang the bell-pull.

Mr Bennett came running in.

'Mr Bennett,' said the professor, sitting back down in his chair. 'These two gentlemen have come from London believing that they have an appointment with me. You handle all my letters. Have I written anything to a Mr Holmes?'

'No, sir,' Mr Bennett answered, going a little red in the face.

'There you are,' said the professor, glaring angrily at Holmes. He pressed his hands firmly onto his desk and leaned forwards. 'It seems to me that you have no right to be here.'

Holmes shrugged his shoulders. 'I can only repeat that I am sorry for the mistake.'

'Sorry is not good enough, Mr Holmes!' shouted the professor in a high, scraping voice. Then he sprang up from his chair and darted towards the door, blocking our exist. He stood there shaking his fists in a furious passion. 'You're not going

to get away with it that easily!'
he cried.

His face stretched into an evil
grin as he continued to shout at us
in a senseless rage. I am sure that
we would have had to fight our

way out of the room if Mr Bennett
had not stepped forwards.

'My dear Professor!' he cried.
'What would the university think
if they heard that you'd been
acting like this? Mr Holmes is
a well-known man. You cannot
treat him with such rudeness!'

Sulkily, the professor stepped
away from the door so that we
could leave. I was very glad to
get out of the house and into the
quiet tree-lined drive.

Holmes, however, seemed to find the whole thing very funny.

'The professor's temper is certainly bad. Perhaps our visit was a little impolite, but we have met him face to face, which is what I wanted,' he said. Suddenly, there came the sound of running feet behind us. 'Dear me, Watson, he is following us!'

But, to my relief, it was not the angry professor who appeared round the bend of the drive, but Mr

Bennett. He came panting up to us.

'I am so sorry, Mr Holmes. I wanted to apologise.'

'Mr Bennett there is no need,' said Holmes. 'It is just another experience in my line of work.'

'I have never seen him in such a dangerous mood,' said Mr Bennett, still getting his breath back. 'He gets angrier by the day. You can understand why Edith and I are so afraid.'

'But his mind is so clear!' said

Holmes. 'That was my mistake. His memory is much better than I thought. By the way, Mr Bennett, may we see the window of Miss Presbury's room?'

Mr Bennett pushed his way through some shrubs and we had a view of the side of the house. 'It is there,' he said, pointing to a high window.

'Dear me, it is impossible to reach,' said Holmes. 'There is some wisteria and ivy growing up

the wall, and you could cling to the drainpipe, but it would still be very difficult to climb.'

'I could not climb it myself,' said Mr Bennett.

Holmes nodded. 'It would be dangerous for any normal man.'

'There was one other thing that I wanted to tell you, Mr Holmes,' said Mr Bennett. 'I have the address of the man who has been sending the professor mysterious letters. The professor must have written to him this morning, as

I was able to read the ink on his

blotting paper and copy it. As his

Blotting paper

A highly absorbent paper used when writing letters. When a letter is first written, the ink from the pen will be very wet. A thick sheet of blotting paper is placed on top of the letter to soak up any excess ink and stop the writing from smudging. Once the blotting paper is taken off, the letter will be dry and ready to be folded and placed into an envelope. Blotting paper is an excellent tool for spying on people, as the paper will take an exact copy of what is written in their letter. Then a detective can read what has been written without the writer of the letter ever knowing.

secretary, I feel bad for spying on him, but what else could I do?'

Mr Bennet handed Holmes a piece of paper. 'Dorak – an unusual name,' Holmes said, before tucking the paper into his pocket. 'Originating from Prague, I imagine. Well, it's an important link in the chain. Watson and I shall return to

Dorak,
Commercial Road,
London

London this afternoon, Mr
Bennett. There is nothing more
for us to do here. We cannot
arrest the professor because he
hasn't committed any crime. No
action is possible at the moment.'

Mr Bennett looked worried.
'Then what on earth can we do?'

'Patience, Mr Bennett. Things
will happen soon – next Tuesday,
in fact, if I'm not mistaken. We
shall be back here in Camford on
that day. I know it will be difficult

until then. Can Miss Presbury stay in London? She will be safer staying away from her father, at least until we solve this mystery.'

'Yes, of course. I'll suggest it to her right away,' said Mr Bennett, looking relieved.

'She must stay there until all danger has passed,' said Holmes. 'Meanwhile, let the professor do what he wants and don't annoy him. As long as he is in a good mood, all will be well.'

Mr Bennett gasped. 'There he is!'

Looking between the branches, we saw the tall figure of the professor come out of the front door and look around. He stood leaning forwards, his hands swinging straight in front of him and his head turning from side to side.

With a final wave, Mr Bennett slipped off among the trees and walked back to join the professor. We watched them go back into the house, the professor frowning and

shouting insults at Mr Bennett

with each step.

Chapter Six

On our way back to the Chequers
Inn, Holmes looked worried. 'I think
the professor has guessed that Mr
Bennett called us in,' he said. 'Poor
Mr Bennett is going to be in trouble.'

We stopped off at the post office
for Holmes to send a telegram.
The reply to it reached us in the
evening. He tossed it to me.

POST OFFICE
TELEGRAM

For free repetition of doubtful words telephone "Telegrams Enquiry" or call, with this form, at office of delivery. Other enquiries should be accompanied by this form and, if possible, the envelope.

Charges to pay
6 s. 5 d
RECEIVED
at Central Telegraph
Office, E.C.I.

Have visited Commercial Road and seen Dorak. He is a smart, polite, elderly person from Prague. He owns a large general shop.
Mercer.

Office of Origin and Service Instructions or Nature of Service, if other than telegram.	Words	Received
Norfolk	23	

'I've only known Mercer since you left Baker Street,' said Holmes. 'He helps me to find out information. He's no Watson, of course.' Holmes turned his head and smiled at me. 'But he did well on this task. It was important to know something about the man the professor writes to. His nationality connects him to the Prague visit.'

'Thank goodness something connects with something,' I said. 'At the moment we seem to have lots of pieces of the puzzle, but none of them fit together. For example, what possible connection could there be between Roy the dog getting angry and a visit to Prague? And what's the link between them and the professor crawling down a hallway at night? As to the dates these things happened on, that's the biggest mystery of all!'

Holmes smiled and rubbed his hands together with glee. We were now seated in the lounge of the old hotel with a coffee in front of each of us.

'Well, let's look at the dates first,' said Holmes, pressing his

fingertips together and speaking
as if he were teaching a class.
'Mr Bennett's excellent diary
shows us that there was trouble
on the 2nd of July. And from

then onwards
something
strange
happened every
nine days, with
only one
exception:
the 5th

of September. It is more than a coincidence.'

I agreed.

'Let us suppose, then, that every nine days the professor takes a strong medicine or maybe even a poison that has a strange effect on him for a short time. It makes him angry and act oddly. And perhaps he took more than his normal dose on the 4th of September, which is why he was still acting strangely the next day.

'It's likely that he learned about this medicine while in Prague and is now supplied with it by the man in London. This could be the answer, Watson!'

'But the dog, the professor's face at the window, and the fact he crawled along the passage – where do those clues fit in?' I asked. 'And why would he take a medicine that makes him so angry and violent?'

'I'm not sure, but we have made a start,' said Holmes. 'I don't expect anything else to happen until next Tuesday. In the meantime, all we can do is to keep in touch with Mr Bennett and enjoy these delicious coffees.' Holmes sipped from his cup and smiled contently.

In the morning, Mr Bennett came round to give us the latest news.

Holmes was right. The professor had guessed that Mr Bennett had asked for our help. Poor Mr Bennett was shouted at for a full hour after we left. This morning, however, the professor was his normal self again and had given a brilliant lecture at the university.

'Apart from the strange episodes,' said Mr Bennett, 'Professor Presbury has more energy than I can ever remember, and his mind is amazingly clear.

Yet he's not the man he used to be.'

'I think he will be all right for a week now,' said Holmes. 'You have nothing to fear. Doctor Watson and I will head back to London now, but we shall meet you here at the same time next Tuesday. On that day, I hope, we will solve the mystery. Meanwhile, keep us posted as to what happens.'

Chapter Seven

I didn't see Holmes at all for the next few days, but on the Monday evening he sent me a short note.

Please meet me at King's Cross Station tomorrow morning for the nine o'clock train to Camford.

Holmes

On the journey, Holmes told me that all was peaceful at the professor's home and his behaviour had been normal.

Later, in our room at the Chequers Inn, Mr Bennett came to see us.

'The professor heard from Dorak, his London agent, this morning,' he said. 'He was sent a letter and a small packet, each

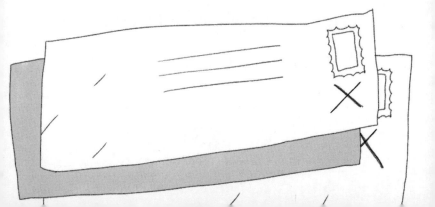

with a cross under the stamp
warning me not to open them.
There has been nothing else.'

'That may be quite enough,'
said Holmes. 'Mr Bennett, I think
we shall get to the bottom of this
mystery tonight. But in order to
do so you must stay awake and
be on the lookout. If you hear
the professor pass your door, do
not interrupt him. Follow him
as quietly as you can. Doctor
Watson and I will not be far off.

By the way, where is the key for the little box you mentioned? The one that the professor hides in his instruments cupboard.'

'On his watch chain,' said Mr Bennett.

'The lock on the cupboard should be easy to break.' Holmes paused and thought for a moment, running over the steps of the plan in his head. 'Well, we can't do anything else until something happens,' he said.

'Goodbye, Mr Bennett. I expect we shall see you before morning.'

It was nearly midnight when Holmes and I took up our positions behind some bushes opposite the front door of Professor Presbury's house.
It was a fine night, but chilly, and we were glad of our warm coats. There was a breeze, and the clouds were drifting steadily

across the sky, hiding the moon
from time to time.

'If the nine-day cycle is correct, the professor should be at his worst tonight,' whispered Holmes. 'These strange symptoms began after his visit to Prague, and every nine days he has received letters from Dorak in London, who has links with Prague. Today he received one of those packages. What kind of medicine it is and why he takes it is still a mystery. But the effect it has is remarkable. Did you see his knuckles?'

'No, I didn't look at them,' I said, surprised.

'They were thick and knobbly. I've never seen anything like it on a human. Always look at the hands first, Watson. Then look at cuffs, trouser-knees, and shoes. The professor's knuckles were extremely curious and can only be explained by …'

Holmes paused and then clapped his hand to his forehead. 'Oh, Watson! Watson, what a fool I have been! It seems incredible, and yet it must be true. How could I miss seeing the connection? Those knuckles! And the dog! And the ivy! There isn't time to explain it now, but–' Holmes gasped and pointed towards the front door. 'Look out, Watson! There he is! You will soon see for yourself what I have just realised.'

The front door had slowly opened. Against the lit

background, we saw the tall figure of Professor Presbury. He was in his dressing gown. As he stood outlined in the doorway, he was upright but leaning forwards with

his arms dangling in front of him, just like when we'd last seen him.

When the professor stepped out onto the drive, an extraordinary change came over him. He sank down into a crouching position and crawled quickly along on his hands and feet. He moved along the front of the house, and then turned round the corner. As he disappeared, Mr Bennett came out of the door and quietly followed him.

'Come, Watson,' whispered Holmes, and we crept as softly as we could through the bushes until we could see the side of the house, bathed in the light of the moon.

The professor was crouching at the foot of the wall. As we watched, he suddenly began to climb up the ivy and wisteria that covered it. He sprang from branch to branch, his feet and hands grasping securely. I could see the joy on his face. With his

dressing gown flapping on each side of him, he looked like a huge bat glued to the side of his house – a great dark patch on the moonlit wall.

Soon the professor became tired of climbing and dropped back down to the ground. He crept towards the stable on his hands and feet.

Roy, the wolfhound, had woken up and left his bed. He barked furiously at the professor and pulled against the chain attached to his collar.

Professor Presbury squatted down just out of reach of the dog and began to tease him in every possible way. He took handfuls of pebbles from the drive and threw them in the dog's face. He prodded him with a stick. He flicked his hands a few centimetres in front of Roy's gaping mouth and tried in every way to anger the poor dog.

In all our adventures, I had never seen a stranger sight than the professor crouching frog-like on the ground

and goading the angry dog that leaped and barked in front of him. It was horrible to watch the innocent creature being tormented.

And then something even worse happened.

Chapter Eight

It was not the chain that broke but the well-worn collar. We heard the sound of the chain hitting the ground, and the next instant Roy and Professor Presbury were rolling on the ground together, one growling in rage and the other screaming in terror.

The professor's life was at

stake. Roy had him by the throat

– his fangs had bitten deep – and

the professor lost consciousness.

Holmes and I darted out from

our hiding place and dragged the

two apart. Mr Bennett was just behind us and ordered Roy to sit.

The uproar had woken the coachman, Mr McPhail. He rushed down from his flat above the stables.

'I'm not surprised,' Mr McPhail said, shaking his head. 'I've seen the professor tormenting Roy before. I knew the dog would get him sooner or later.'

When Roy had calmed down and was tied up by his bed again,

we carried the professor into the house and up to his room. Mr Bennett helped me put a dressing on the professor's badly bleeding throat and give him an injection for the pain. He sank into a deep sleep. Only then were we able to look at each other and think about the strange event that had just happened.

'I think a skilled surgeon needs to see the professor,' I said. 'He's badly injured.'

'For heaven's sake, no!'
exclaimed Mr Bennett. 'We
don't want the scandal to spread
outside this house. Imagine what
would happen if the university
found out how the professor
has been acting. Think how his
daughter would feel!'

'Quite so,' said Holmes. 'I
think it might be possible to keep
the matter to ourselves and to
prevent it happening again. Could
I have the key from the watch-

chain, please, Mr Bennett? Mr McPhail will guard the patient and let us know if there is any change. Let's see what we can find in the professor's precious box.'

There was not much, but there was enough. There was a tiny bottle of liquid and a syringe for injecting it. There was also an empty bottle and several letters in messy handwriting. The crosses under the stamps on the envelopes showed that they were the ones that Mr Bennett had been told not to open. Each one was sent from Commercial Road

and signed "A. Dorak". They were bills and receipts.

There was one other envelope that Holmes picked out. It was written in neater handwriting. It had a foreign stamp and was postmarked Prague.

'Here we have it!' cried Holmes as he pulled the letter out of the envelope.

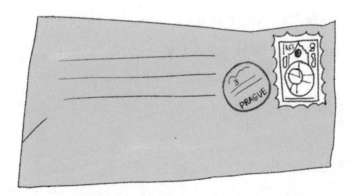

Honoured colleague,

Since your visit I have thought a lot about your case. The medicine I have given you is very effective, but I would advise you to be cautious. The results can be dangerous.

It is possible that the Anthropoid serum would be better. As I explained to you, I have used Black-Faced Langur serum in this medicine. Langur is, of course, a crawler and a climber, while Anthropoid walks upright and is more human-like.

I beg you to be very careful. Please send Mr Dorak, my agent in England, weekly reports of how you are doing.

Yours faithfully,

H. Lowenstein

Lowenstein! I knew that name! I'd seen something in the newspaper about a scientist who was developing a serum to make people look and act younger and live longer. His strength-giving serum was denied by doctors because he refused to say what was in it.

I told Holmes and Mr Bennett about the article. 'So now we know,' I said. 'The professor is using a serum taken from monkeys.'

Mr Bennett took a book of zoology from a shelf. 'Langur,' he read, 'the great black-faced monkey of the Himalayan slopes.

The biggest and most human of climbing monkeys.' He looked up. 'Well, thanks to you, Mr Holmes, it is very clear that we have traced the evil to its source: this dangerous medicine.'

Holmes shook his head. 'The real source is the love affair between the professor and his younger fiancée. He clearly tried to turn himself into a much younger man for her. When one tries to rise above nature, one is likely to fall below it.'

Holmes sat holding the little bottle of greenish liquid in his hand for a while. He stared at it thoughtfully. 'I shall write to Lowenstein and tell him that he is

criminally responsible for sending
out these poisons,' he said.

Holmes then sprang to his feet.
'Well, I think there is nothing
more to be said, Mr Bennett. Roy
the dog was clearly aware of the
change in the professor before you
were. His sense of smell made sure
of that. It was the monkey, not
the professor, that Roy attacked.
Just as it was the monkey that
teased Roy and the monkey that
climbed the wall. Climbing was a

joy to him. I'm sure that it was by pure chance that he reached Miss Presbury's window.

'I will personally make sure that Mr Lowenstein stops sending these dangerous potions to the people of England. Doctor Watson and I shall find a discreet surgeon to treat Professor Presbury – one who will keep your secret.'

Holmes turned towards me and smiled. 'There's an early morning train to London, Watson. I think we shall just have time for a cup of tea at the Chequers Inn before we catch it.'

Sherlock Holmes

World-renowned private detective Sherlock Holmes has solved hundreds of mysteries, and is the author of such fascinating monographs as *Early English Charters* and *The Influence of a Trade Upon the Form of a Hand*. He keeps bees in his free time.

Dr John Watson

Wounded in action at Maiwand, Dr John Watson left the army and moved into 221B Baker Street. There he was surprised to learn that his new friend, Sherlock Holmes, faced daily peril solving crimes, and began documenting his investigations. Dr Watson also runs a doctor's practice.

To download Sherlock Holmes activities, please visit www.sweetcherrypublishing.com/resources